8/15/05 5:55

To Mrs Michele

From Mrs Harris.

I hope you enjoy reading it to the Children.

/s

The Adventures of Fred Tom-Tom and His Farm Friends

Book One

Evelynn

VANTAGE PRESS
New York

To my mother, Mrs. Birdie Davis; my brother, Mr. Colie Davis; my daughters and their spouses: Denise and Darren, Daphne and Edward; my sons and their spouses: Gregory and Sherri, Percy and Joanne; and Bryan. To my grandchildren, aunt, uncle, cousins, in-laws, and Kimila.

To my professors at Rider: Drs. Ahia, Guindon, Murphy, Stein, and Kavanaugh. Mr. Kimble, principal, colleagues at Holland Middle School, and Mr. Rawlins, my "good buddy."

To my church family, neighbors, and friends.

With special appreciation and thanks to my ancestors.

Special thanks to my typist, Mrs. Shirley C. Wright.

Finally, to the memory of my two deceased daughters: Marsha Anne Coulter and Vernessa Michelle Coulter-Poe.

Contents

Foreword

When Evelynn asked me to write this Foreword, I was touched; touched not only by the request itself but by the form in which it came. She included it in a thank-you letter to me. As Evelynn's professor, I was being thanked for just doing my job, for training her to become a professional counselor. While all of the counseling services faculty at Rider have contributed to her skill development, the truth is, when she came to us, she already had the two attributes most needed in a helping professional: a good, caring heart and the will to make a difference even when others have given up. She has made, is making, and will continue to make a real difference in the lives of those who need it the most. Like Tom-Tom, she has led others in her community to their own kind of freedom, however each of them may envision it, and she has done this best by the example she sets. Evelynn has accomplished in her own life what many have been afraid to try.

Evelynn lives her life knowing that each of us is responsible for our own freedom and for finding our own way no matter how dire our present environment or how hard the path ahead. Her special gift is the ability to see beyond current circumstances to hidden potential. She provides inspiration and tangible, concrete means to accomplish goals. Wherever there is a need she offers help and hope. She extends her hand to the neglected child, the confused teen, the overwhelmed young mother, the overburdened middle-aged woman, or the family in disarray.

Through Harris House Community Services Programs and Harris House, Inc., Evelynn practices what Tom-Tom teaches us in this little book. She has been unable to sleep through the long night of drugs, alcohol, or joblessness destroying too many of our families. She calls us to awaken and leads the way to freedom through responsible action. She epitomizes these words of Councillor Mandizvidza of Zimbabwe:

> Women have solved the problems of human life from embryo to birth and from birth to maturity. Women are the survival kit of the human race.

By purchasing this book you have become part of the survival kit. Proceeds from its sale will contribute to a plan to bring professional counseling services for families in the inner city of Trenton, New Jersey.

Enjoy Tom-Tom's story with the children in your life. And after you have done so, join Evelynn in her vision for a better community.

—Mary H. Guindon, Ph.D.
  Associate Professor, Counseling Services
  Department of Graduate Education & Human Services
  College of Liberal Arts, Education & Sciences
  Rider University
  Lawrenceville, New Jersey

The Adventures of Fred Tom-Tom
and
His Farm Friends

1
The Sale

Late one balmy night, Fred Tom-Tom was awakened by his recurring dream of being cooked for a special occasion. Unable to sleep, he decided to go for a walk.

He didn't know exactly when this special occasion was going to take place, but he felt it would be very soon.

Sally Hen had warned all the barnyard animals about eating extra portions of food. She told them that this usually meant that they were being fattened for a special occasion, with them as the main course. Ever since Sally Hen had made that statement, Fred had become more watchful.

Fred became very concerned one morning when he noticed Mr. Hale giving him an extra portion of corn. Mr. Hale even picked him up and felt his chest and legs. As Sally had warned, this meant he was going to be cooked very soon.

Fred thought that going for a nice long walk

1

might help clear his head and help him sleep. Not wanting to burden his sleeping friends with his problem, he decided to walk quietly down to the meadow, sit under the huge willow tree, and think.

As he started walking across the barnyard, Fred noticed lights on in the master bedroom. He wondered what could possibly be going on this time of night to keep the family up this late, because Mr. and Mrs. Hale usually retired very early to bed. Curious to find out, Fred cautiously ambled toward the big house, making sure not to arouse the two ferocious German Shepherds, asleep under the huge pecan trees in the back yard.

Quickly, without making a sound, Fred made his way toward the house. Once in the crawl space under the house, he stuck his neck high between the beams of the house, right under the master bedroom.

He heard Mr. Hale talking to Mrs. Hale. "We have made the right decision to sell the farm, honey. I can no longer keep up with my daily chores.

"I get tired much faster now. The doctor warned me to take it easy and relax more, because the stress and strain of everyday farming is too much for my heart."

"I know," said Mrs. Hale. "My back and hands are giving me problems too. I can no longer do my housework. It takes me forever to complete a simple

task with no one to help us, and with no money coming in, I feel it is best that we sell the farm now while we can still obtain a good price for it."

"Yes," said Mr. Hale. "The men from the poultry and livestock organization will be coming early in the morning to buy the farm animals. I made sure that each animal was given enormous amounts of food to eat, so they will look healthy and plump when the men come to buy them."

"That is good, honey," said Mrs. Hale. "Now turn off the light so we can get some sleep. Morning will be here before we know it."

"Oh!" said Fred, almost hitting his head on the beams as he turned to leave. *They are going to sell us in the morning,* he thought. *What shall we do? What shall we do?* Hurrying back to the barn, Fred almost fell over the sleeping dogs. His face and neck were hot; his body felt like an oven with him inside, and his feet felt like two red-hot coals.

Once safely inside the barn, Fred began awakening all the cows, pigs, chickens, ducks, goats, rabbits, and horses. He told them what he had heard. The cows and goats said, "We will not give any more milk. Then they will not be able to sell us."

The chickens and ducks said, "We will not give any more eggs."

"Yes," said the rabbits and pigs, "we will look

really sick and lie down when they come to take us away."

"They will not buy us if we are sick," said the goats.

"That might not work," said Fred. "Suppose we aren't convincing enough. We must think of a better plan. A plan that will not fail."

Each animal began to think and think and think and think.

"Oh," said Fred, "we must come up with an answer very soon, because it is almost morning."

"Yes," said the rooster, "and I will have to go crow in the new day."

"I can't think of anything," was the reply from each animal. "I guess we will have to keep our original plan. It might work or it might not work," said a pig. "It is the only plan we have."

Suddenly, Fred began to smile. The other farm animals all chimed in at once. "Tell us your plan, tell us your plan."

"I know what we could do," said Fred, "I know exactly what we could do. This plan just might work."

"Tell us quickly," said the cows. "You know how we dislike being disturbed. We are contented animals and we would like to remain as such. Please don't keep us in suspense. It is simply not healthy for our nerves."

"Yes," said the goats. "Hurry up," said the chickens.

"Don't keep it a secret," quacked the ducks.

"That's right," cried the rabbits and pigs.

"If you have a plan better than our original plans, that will save everyone, please don't keep us in suspense," said the rooster. "Our lives depend on having a plan that will work. Tell us your plan before I am forced by nature to crow in the new day. You know what happens when I do that. The entire farm becomes a beehive of activity."

Fred opened his mouth hesitatingly. All the animals stood closely together, eager to hear his plan. The plan he felt would save them from being sold.

The animals wondered, *What plan could a silly old washed out turkey have and how could his plan possibly save a whole barnyard of frightened and desperate animals?*

2
The Plan

Fred moved quickly and confidently to the center of the group. His legs moved with the stride of someone fully in control. He knew his plan would work. He knew his plan was the better plan. He must now use his best salesmanship skills if he wants the group to choose his plan. Fred's delivery must be perfect; voice strong and convincing. This was going to be the performance of his life. Come to think of it, the lives of all the animals rested on his shoulders. Now he must reveal to the others why their plans wouldn't work.

Standing firmly in the center of the group, Fred stated, "The plans each of you conveyed to the group are not workable."

"Why?" quacked the ducks.

"Yes, why?" squealed the pigs.

"We feel our combined plans should work," mooed the cows.

"We all had ample time to think of a workable plan," clucked the chickens.

"But all we have to show for our thinking is a headache," cried the goats.

"Yes," mooed the cows, "a headache."

"If you have a better plan, please tell us. I have only a few more minutes before I must go to work," said the rooster.

"This is my plan," said Fred, putting his right foot firmly in front of his left foot. "We must run away, immediately! If we stay, our performances might not be convincing and we will all lose our lives. These people are not coming to keep us for eggs, milk, butter, cheese, feathers, hides, or furs. They are coming to take our lives. They intend to sell our meat."

"Yes," grunted the pigs. "We never thought they would harm us."

"We must leave right now," said Fred, "before the dogs wake up and start their daily routine of chasing us around the barnyard. You know how mean and playful they become once we are let out in the morning to stretch our legs. They appear to really enjoy chasing us around and around until we become tired, frustrated, and angry. Their madness usually continues until we finally give up and make our way wearily back into the barn."

"Let us put it to a fast vote," commanded Sally

the hen. "Those in favor of going with Fred, stand behind Fred. Those in favor of the first group of plans simply remain where you are."

It took only a few minutes for all the farm animals to agree to follow Fred. Each quickly and quietly took his or her place behind Fred. "Well, Fred," replied Sally Hen, "I guess since this is your plan, you are our leader for now."

"Well wait," neighed the horses.

"No one asked us if we wanted to leave. I guess you assumed we wanted to remain on the farm because we may not be eliminated for food. Grant you, we might not lose our lives, but we are tired of pulling, hauling, and standing in the searing sun. This arduous work is making us sick. With all of you gone, things will not be the same. If someone would open the barn doors, we would like to tag along with you," said George, the senior horse.

"Okay," commanded Fred, "We must leave right now. There is no time to waste. This is the plan. We shall form a single line. I will be leading you, through the meadow, across the lake, past the willow trees, around the orchard, and straight into Mr. Hale's woods. I would like Sally Hen to bring up the rear."

Fred opened the barn door quietly and each animal swiftly passed through without making any unnecessary noise. Fred led the way with Sally Hen bringing up the rear.

The night air felt soft and warm as it caressed gently the bodies of this frightened group. Behind the east fields, a slight tint of the morning sun could be vaguely seen, cautiously making its early morning entrance.

Fred and his group moved swiftly. Soon, they entered the luscious green meadow. "Make sure to walk in the lake. This will cover our scent and tracks. Hopefully this method will keep the dogs from locating us," said Fred.

"Move faster," commanded Sally. "I want to put as much distance between me and that farm as possible."

"Yes," whispered the rooster very, very gently. "They will soon be wondering why I haven't stood on that silly old weather beaten fence post and crowed in the morning."

"Hurry, hurry, the lake is straight ahead," conveyed Fred to the group. "Once on the other side of the lake, past the orchard, I think we will be able to breathe a sigh of relief. We will be safe once we are in the woods."

"Woods are usually dark and deep. I feel we will be safe once we are there. Let's stop talking, we need all our strength just to keep walking. The sun will soon be up, and we all know how unbearably hot it usually becomes on this tract of land," informed Sally Hen.

Suddenly, slumbering misty morning gave way to bright sunshine, with the sun quickly taking command, gently burning off the dew, quietly dispelling the darkness, and slowly bringing warmth and movement to the once sleepy morning.

Not a whisper could be heard as the animals quietly and obediently followed their leader. What a sight they made. Looking dejected though determined, this group of misfits kept marching forward. Everyone was hoping and dreaming of a better life, a life far away from the drudgery they were once forced to endure.

Each animal stayed with their particular group and obeyed the leader's directions. No one complained, made unnecessary noise, became unmanageable, or disgruntled with their leader's commands.

Each respected the other and wanted only to make the plan work. Fred was their leader. His plan had been chosen and everyone agreed to follow his lead.

Inwardly, each animal had determined to make Fred's plan work. No one would seek to sabotage the plan. They would not think about turning back, complaining, or murmuring if things became a little rough. Each had chosen to come along willingly in search of a better and safer life.

The woods could be seen in the immediate

distance. Everyone wanted to shout, but remembering Fred's warning, they held their peace and waited for the appropriate time to voice their jubilance.

There were approximately a thousand yards to cover before they would be safely in the woods. Fred was leading beautifully, but suddenly and without warning, he stopped. His long neck shot up quickly. Everyone quickly came to an abrupt halt.

The horses almost trampled the little band of ducks. "A close call," neighed the horses as they reared up on their hind legs.

"What did Fred hear that would cause him to stop so abruptly?" clucked the chickens.

"Quiet!" squealed the pigs softly. "We are not to talk."

"But," questioned the goats, "what is going on up front to make Fred stop? Aren't we almost to our destination?"

"Be quiet," commanded Sally Hen.

"We are afraid," sniffed the rabbits softly. "Maybe there are hunters up ahead," uttered the goats. "If this is true," mooed the cows gingerly, "we have jumped from the frying pan into the fire."

"We didn't leave the farm to get caught by some hunters. This is really a fine kettle of fish we have gotten ourselves into now," said the ducks.

"Be quiet," declared Sally, "whatever is up ahead

couldn't possibly be any worse than what Mr. Hale had planned for us."

"I beg to differ with you," quacked the ducks. "We feel that there might be something up ahead worse than what Mr. Hale had planned for us."

3
In the Woods

The weight of being the leader rested heavily upon Fred's shoulders. He fully understood his mission. As Fred walked steadily forward, he prayed for strength, an understanding heart, courage to keep moving forward, and the ability to be an effective leader.

He knew he had not had the pleasure of leading out in any projects or activities when he lived on the farm. But now, while walking ahead of the group, he wondered if he was the right one for the job. Did he have what it took to be a leader? How does one become a leader? Are leaders born? Do they go to school to learn how to become a leader? Maybe something happened to cause an individual to become a leader at a precise moment. Fred could not remember how leaders came about, but for now, he would do his best to lead until the real leader stepped forward.

Fred didn't want to make any mistakes. A mistake could be fatal for everyone. He quickly regained his composure and returned to the job at hand of listening attentively to the various sounds emitting from the woods.

A particular fowl or animal was making every sound emitting from the woods—animals and fowl he lived among until captured by Mr. Hale and forced to live on his farm. The farm life domesticated him to a point, but still running through his warm blood were fragments of his wild heritage. These wild fragments lingered within his body and refused to go away quietly because Fred fought to retain them. Fred was not totally domesticated or totally wild. He simply refused to become completely domesticated, because he wanted someday to be wild once again.

In the recesses of Fred's mind ran the hope of one day being able to return to his family and former way of life. His roots. He did not appreciate what he once had, until it was taken from him. As a wild turkey, he had many freedoms, but on the farm, Fred's beautiful feathers and claws were constantly being clipped to keep him from flying away to freedom. Oh, how Fred yearned to be free once again! Free to roam the many hills, explore the numerous caves, swim in the clear cool streams and lakes, fly from tree to tree, run through the green meadows, smell the sweet fragrance's from the many colorful flowers, and eat fresh berries and other fruit that surrounded his beautiful home. Oh!

How he wanted to be free once again. Free to feel the wind beneath his wings as he soared high above the earth. Fred felt sad about what he had done to cause him to lose his freedom. He was sorry Mr. Hale had slightly domesticated him. He loved living wild in the woods with his mother, father, two sisters, and three brothers. Fred didn't know what had become of them, but he was not going to allow himself to be captured again if he could help it.

Fred wondered if his family was still alive or had they been captured and taken far away. "Maybe they were all sold or worse," thought Fred as he continued walking toward the woods with his band of misfits marching along behind.

Clearing his mind of his previous thoughts, Fred led on.

The luscious green woods quietly reached out its long leafy arms of love and welcomed the entire group, enveloping them snugly, gently, and deeply into its fortress of trees, shrubbery, fowl, animals, smells, and numerous sounds.

Once safely inside the woods, Fred told the group to stop and take a break. They had been traveling for some time without stopping to eat or drink, and Fred felt that a good long rest was needed.

The rabbits, horses, pigs, goats, chickens, and other animals quickly began nibbling on the luscious green grass and assortment of berries and fruits that abundantly arrayed the entrance to the woods.

While everyone was busily eating, Sally Hen pushed forward to ask Fred why he had suddenly decided to stop when they were about one thousand yards away from the safety of the woods. "Yes," chimed several other weary animals, "why did you stop? Did you sense danger ahead, did you see or hear something that you felt would mean sudden disaster for us?"

"We would like to hear also," sniffed the rabbits, as they all stopped eating and snuggled closely against Fred's feet.

"Was there someone or something ahead that caused you to stop so suddenly?" questioned Sally Hen.

"Sit down everyone," uttered Fred, "I will tell you how I came to be a prisoner on the Hale Farm."

Each animal quickly secured a soft seat on the luscious cool green grass. Each wanted to hear what Fred, their leader, had to say.

"Speak," whinnied the horses.

"Okay, here goes," replied Fred. "Whenever you are in an unfamiliar area or you sense danger, take a few minutes and study the area around you very carefully before making your next move. Listen for anything that might give you a clue as to what is going on around you or ahead of you. Use your five senses thoroughly to help you decide your next move, because your life could depend on it. It pays to be very careful. Don't play with your life. Life is worth living and you should want to live a long, happy, and productive life.

"That's enough teaching for now. On with the story," said Fred.

"When we were approaching the woods, I stopped suddenly to allow my eyes a chance to scan the immediate perimeter. My eyes were searching for anything unfamiliar or something out of place and my keen ears were listening to the various sounds emitting from the woods. Each sound is distinct and I wanted to know what each meant and whom they belonged to. Remember, I grew up in these woods. Here is where I lived with my family before being captured and it all happened because I wouldn't listen to my parents. They couldn't tell me anything. I thought I knew everything about everything. Boy, how wrong I was. My mother and father warned me about my cocky disposition, but what they were trying to tell me and warn me about made no sense at all to me then. I felt they were simply trying to keep me from having fun. I also felt they wanted me to sit around the house with them and not to enjoy my life. Besides, I really believed that nothing bad would ever happen to me," sighed Fred sadly.

"My life was my own and I didn't want to hear

another lecture or warning about safety. Life is to be lived, so why were my parents trying to keep me from living my own life? They were old and seemed not interested in having fun but I wanted to travel, see new places, make new friends, and choose my own paths. They, on the other hand, wanted me to go slowly and enjoy the many things around me, but I wanted more, lots more. How was I ever going to enjoy life if they constantly kept warning me to be careful and to come straight home after school?

"Daily, my parents spoke to us about safety and following their advice. Many times I ran from the house to escape another lecture. Warnings, warnings, warnings were a part of our daily life and I was tired of it. My parent's lectures and warnings didn't seem to bother my brothers or sisters. They appeared to welcome our parents' advice, and seemed unconcerned about being free to make their own decisions.

"But, I wanted to be free. Free to make my own decisions. Free to control my own destiny. Free to choose my own friends, and most of all I wanted to be free of my meddling parents' restrictions, and lectures. Now I see how wrong my thinking really was.

"I can still remember that ill-fated morning. Mother was in the kitchen preparing breakfast and needed some more wood for the kitchen stove and a quart of blueberries for the pancakes. My father asked me to collect the wood from the woodpile for the kitchen stove and to pick the quart of blueberries.

"Work, work, work, was all I could remember. There was always something that needed doing around the house. I never seemed to have enough time for myself, or to play with my friends. If I was not doing work around the house, I was busy with my homework. Each teacher seemed eager to give lots of homework. To me it appeared that all adults wanted to do was to keep me from having fun and being happy. How was I ever going to have any real fun and be happy if I was constantly being overloaded with housework and homework? Keeping your room clean, taking out the garbage, sweeping the floors, raking leaves, cutting and stacking wood for the stoves, gathering wood for the stoves, drawing water from the well, planting seeds in the garden, weeding the garden, watering the garden and gathering the vegetables from the garden, collecting eggs from the chickens, berries and other fruit from the various trees and bushes, washing the dog, and dusting the furniture were just a few of my many chores. Life in the country as a young turkey just didn't seem fair. There was too much work to be done and not enough free time for me to really enjoy my friends. So I thought.

"After school at Mrs. Goose's one-room

schoolhouse on that ill-fated Friday afternoon, I headed home grudgingly. Mrs. Goose had given me three pages of mathematics, twenty spelling words to define, identify the parts of speech, write two sentences for each word and an English Literature paper to rewrite over the short weekend. How would I be able to have any free time with all this homework staring me in the face?

"I needed time to think, so I took the long way home. The long way led pass a large clear cold lake. Soon I was at the lake and in the water.

"The water was nice and cold, the sun was scorching hot on my feathers and my mind was free of all life's many problems, my parents lectures, and schoolwork. For once in my life, I was free to do as I pleased. There was no one around to interfere with my having fun. Yes, I remembered the swimming safety rules, but I ignored them and went on trying several very dangerous and difficult swimming strokes and dives.

"My swimming coach had warned everyone about trying new swimming strokes and dives without proper supervision and training, but I didn't want to heed his warning at this time. I wanted to do my own thing regardless of the warnings. Everything was going great for a while but quickly things began to change.

"All at once it seemed to grow dark. Jumping

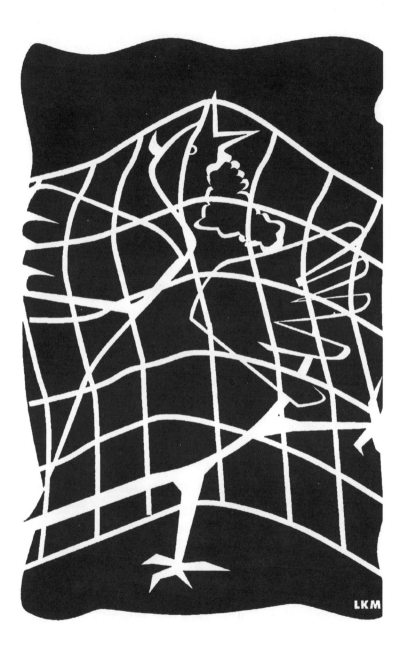

quickly out of the water, I shook myself dry, picked up my many books, and headed toward home. I was in such a hurry to get home I forgot what my parents told me numerous times about being careful when walking alone, especially, when walking in unfamiliar territory. I didn't see the huge black net hanging in the tall trees above my path as I turned the corner in the woods.

"All at once, I felt what appeared to be a huge spider web covering my feathers. Desperately, I tried to fly, but my wings were unable to move from my side. Trying to run also proved fruitless. My legs simply became entangled in the huge spider web. The weight of the web kept me from doing anything.

"Soon three men emerged from behind some bushes. Two men carried a large metal box and the third man gently untangled me from the web and placed me in the metal box. I never saw my parents, brothers, sisters, friends, coach, or Mrs. Goose again."

"One day I was happy and free, living in the woods with my family and friends, the next day I was living on a small farm with many smelly animals and an old man and his wife," sighed Fred.

After the story was told, the goats said, "Well, it never hurts to play it safe. If these were the very woods you were captured in, it was truly wise to check every sound and every movement very

carefully before venturing further. You can never be too careful."

"I have learned over these many years not to become overanxious to proceed into uncertainty without first checking things out very carefully," said Fred.

Suddenly, Fred stopped talking, and began listening attentively to some approaching sounds. He motioned for the animals to hide quickly because the sounds were almost upon them. Who were those people? Were they hunters sent by Mr. Hale to bring them back or were they hunters out for a day of animal hunting? Whoever they were, Fred felt they spelled trouble, the kind of trouble that could quickly turn an animal into a meal or a trophy. Either way was unacceptable by the group.

"Hurry," commanded Fred, "hide, hide, hide, I sense trouble. I sense big trouble."

4
Friend or Foe

The chickens, pigs, and ducks hurried toward the luscious tall green bushes that stood in abundance just ahead of them, while the others took cover behind several large stately rocks. Each animal quickly began to concentrate on the approaching sounds that kept getting closer and closer. But it was Fred who recognized at once that these approaching hunters were young people. He could tell by their voices that they were a group of young people but he was unable to detect if they were friend or foe. If they had been sent by Mr. Hale to return them up to the farm or if they were simply out for a walk in the woods.

They didn't sound like eager hunters, but what would they be doing in these woods this time of the day, if they weren't hunters? pondered Fred.

Closer and still closer the group came. Faster and still faster beat each animal's heart. Breathing softly and quietly, each animal tried desperately not to make a sound that would alert the young people to their hiding places.

"Rita, I didn't realize when we moved from the city to the country that gathering wood for the stoves would be so arduous. I thought it would be fun."

"Yes, the task is arduous, and not a fun thing I like doing, but let's get the job completed. Besides, we only have this assignment for one week, then we will be given a new assignment provided we accomplish this chore well," conveyed Keisha.

"Okay, Keisha, I get the picture. The five of us must keep our present jobs for one week and if they have been completed well, we will each be given a different job the following week," replied James.

"That is correct. Now let's stop talking and get busy. Gathering wood can be a lot of fun for a city dweller turned country farmer," chimed Keisha, "if you put your mind to it."

"Fun!" exclaimed Brian.

"Yes, fun," repeated Keisha. "When I lived in the city, the only trees I saw were in the park, on television, or during a ride with my family in the country once a year to visit my sick grandparents, who later died. The farm was later sold. We returned several times to the old homestead, just to walk through the woods, but there were signs posted along the way prohibiting anyone from entering."

"Oh, boy," said Brian, "how I hated to see those

private property signs; it appears as if a small group of people controls the best parcels of woods and they don't want to share them with anyone."

"I lived on a farm for one summer with ten other students from my school. It was hard work, but I enjoyed it. There were a few farms that had private property signs posted. We were told by our counselors to avoid those woods because they were private property and we might get into trouble if we ventured there," conveyed James.

"Things are really different now," revealed Brian.

"We now have our own woods. Our woods are filled with everything: lakes, streams, meadows, orchards, hills, caves, animals, birds, and many, many more wonderful and exciting things. Our group owns one thousand acres of these beautiful woods, and we are free to walk unrestricted through every foot of these woods. I also like the name of our village, it has a safe sound to it," conveyed Keisha.

"Yes, Sanctuary Village does have a safe soothing ring to it," agreed James.

"I agree," said Rita. "But let's hurry and gather the wood before it gets dark and we become lost in our woods. You know I am a city girl and I can't see once it becomes dark."

"Come on gang, let's hurry," yelled Brian, "or I will miss my television program, *Little House on the Prairie.*"

"*Little House on the Prairie?*" asked Keisha.

"What's wrong with that?" questioned Brian. "It's a good country show and I have learned a lot about farming by watching that show."

"Don't tease him, Keisha," replied Rita, "because I also enjoy watching the show. It shows how difficult yet enjoyable country living can be."

"Okay, okay, I'm sorry about what I said, so let's hurry so we all can watch the show," replied Keisha.

"I thought they would never leave," whispered Fred.

"Me too," uttered Sally Hen, as she flew from her hiding place.

A sweet sigh of relief could be heard coming from the animals. Their location for the moment had not been jeopardized. But how long could they expect to hide out before they are discovered and made into a scrumptious meal or trophies by some quick trigger-fingered hunters?

With the present danger abated, Fred quickly turned his attention to other immediate needs for the night; shelter, food, and water, while the others sat wondering about being captured. They knew that the size of the woods could spell relief or danger.

Sad to say, they didn't have very long to wait for their answer. For at that very moment, deep in the recesses of the dark woods, sat a small group of eager young hunters planning their strategy for the next day.